D0606917

RUDOLFO ANAYA

Farolitos
for
Abuelo

ILLUSTRATED BY EDWARD GONZALES

HYPERION BOOKS FOR CHILDREN/NEW YORK

FIRST EDITION

1 3 5 7 9 10 8 6 4 2

The artwork was prepared using oil paint.

This book is set in 18/24-point Garamond 3.

Printed in Hong Kong by South China Printing Company Ltd.

LIBRARY OF CONGRESS CATALOGING-IN-PUBLICATION DATA

Anaya, Rudolfo A.

Farolitos for Abuelo / Rudolfo Anaya ; illustrated by Edward Gonzales.

—1st ed.

p.   cm.

Summary: When Luz's beloved grandfather dies, she places luminaria around his grave on Christmas Eve as a way of remembering him.

ISBN 0-7868-0237-5 (trade : alk. paper).

ISBN 0-7868-2186-8 (lib. bdg. : alk. paper).

[1. Grandfathers—Fiction. 2. Death—Fiction. 3. Mexican Americans—Fiction. 4. Christmas—Fiction. 5. New Mexico—Fiction.]

I. Gonzales, Edward, 1947–   ill. II. Title.

PZ7.A5186Fap   1998

[Fic]—dc21   97-46710

Luz awoke and looked out the window. Storm after storm had swept across the Sangre de Cristo Mountains this winter, leaving the village of San Juan snuggled under a blanket of snow. Thin columns of smoke rose from the chimneys of the neighboring houses.

Luz dressed, then hurried to put kindling in the kitchen stove. Soon a fire roared to life, and she put the coffeepot on.

Her abuelo came in the back door with a load of firewood in his arms, which he dropped into the wood box.

"Buenos dias te de Dios, mi'jita," he greeted Luz.

"Buenos dias, Abuelo," Luz said.

She went to her grandfather and gave him a kiss on his cheek. "Your coffee will be ready soon."

"Ah, gracias." The old man thanked her.

Luz always made coffee for her abuelo in the morning. This was a special time of the day they loved to share. By the time her parents got up, the kitchen was nice and cozy.

"You and your abuelo are a great team," Luz's father said as they ate breakfast.

Luz smiled. Abuelo winked.

That afternoon when Luz returned from school, she sat by her abuelo and he helped her with her homework.

"I'm ready for spring," Luz said as she put her books away.

"It's been a long, cold winter," Abuelo agreed. "But already the days are growing longer and warmer. Soon the snow on the mountain peaks will melt and the river will rise. When the earth thaws we can plant our garden."

Every spring Luz and her abuelo planted a garden of corn, chile, squash, and tomatoes. Luz's mother would cook the vegetables for their meals.

"And we can go fishing," Luz said.

"Yes." Abuelo smiled.

Luz loved to go fishing with her grandfather. Every spring they were the first ones on the river.

Just as Abuelo foretold, the snow on the mountain soon began to melt and the river began to rise. The grass grew green and buds were ready to burst on the apple trees.

On the first warm day, Luz found her abuelo digging for worms in the garden. "Time to go fishing," he said.

"Yes!" Luz shouted and ran to pack a lunch.

There were still spots of snow under the shade of the pine trees as they followed the path by the river up the mountain.

They arrived at their favorite fishing spot and sat on the bank of the roaring river. In an hour they had caught three large rainbow trout.

"I love spring," Luz said.

"Spring follows winter," Abuelo said. "Each season has a purpose. In winter the earth is at rest. In spring the earth comes alive."

While they were eating their lunch, four boys from the village came running up the path.

"Hi, Luz," they called. "Catch anything?"

Luz showed them the trout.

"Hey, let's fish," Carlos, one of the boys, called to his friends.

"Nah, let's play!" Ernesto replied, pointing to a huge dead tree that lay across the river. He grabbed a stick and leaped on the tree.

"I dare you to cross," he said, taunting Carlos.

"Out of my way!" Carlos shouted back. He, too, picked up a dry branch, and started toward Ernesto.

Standing on the log in the middle of the rushing water, they began a mock sword fight. The other boys cheered them on.

"Be careful!" Abuelo shouted, but it was too late.

Just as the old man spoke, Carlos slipped and plunged into the cold water. The swift current swept him away.

"Help!" the boys called. "Carlos fell! Help!"

Abuelo quickly ran along the bank of the river with Luz close behind him. When they came to a clearing, Abuelo jumped into the water and grabbed Carlos by the collar. Together they tumbled in the deep current until Abuelo grabbed some tree roots and pulled them both out.

"Go get help," Abuelo gasped, and Luz turned and ran.

She had never run so fast in her life. She raced to the village store where some of the villagers were gathered. They responded to her cries and followed her to the scene of the accident.

The men covered Carlos and Abuelo with their jackets. Both had to be carried home. Carlos was safe, but by the time the men got Abuelo home he was stiff with cold. Luz's mother put him to bed immediately and brought him hot tea to drink.

That night Abuelo had a high fever. By morning he could barely breathe. The doctor came and gave him some medicine, but Abuelo didn't respond. The cold turned to pneumonia.

"Abuelo is dying," Luz's father and mother explained.

"No!" Luz cried. "He can't die!"

She went to her abuelo's bedside and held his hand.

"Don't die, Abuelo," she cried.

"Mi hija," he said in a hoarse whisper. "Remember, there is a purpose to every season. In the spring the trees bloom, in the winter they go to sleep. Once I was young and strong as a tree. Now it is time for me to rest. Just remember I will always be with you."

Luz hugged him tight and told him she loved him.

That night Abuelo died. The neighbors came to say a rosary. They stayed all night with Luz's family and prayed for Abuelo. The women brought food for the mourners. They filled the kitchen table with pots of beans, posole, roasts, red chile, and tortillas. The people remembered all the good things Luz's grandfather had done for the village.

Luz sat by the coffin. She was very sad, but she thought about what her grandfather had told her. It was time for him to rest.

The following day they buried Abuelo in the camposanto by the church. They buried him next to his wife, who had died many years before.

The last few weeks of school were difficult for Luz. Although she kept busy helping her mother, the days seemed empty without Abuelo.

That summer Luz worked hard in her abuelo's garden. She pulled weeds, hoed around the tender plants, and watered them every day, just as her grandfather had taught her.

In the fall, school started again. Luz gathered the vegetables, and when the frost came the plants withered and died.

December came and everyone in the village prepared for Christmas. The boys went up the mountain to cut trees. The priest got the villagers together to present *Los Pastores*, the nativity play they performed every year.

In *Los Pastores* some of the villagers dressed as shepherds going to Bethlehem. On Christmas Eve they walked down the village road on their way to church. They always stopped at Abuelo's house. Last Christmas, Luz and Abuelo had lit farolitos for them.

"I want to do something special for Abuelo," Luz told her parents the morning before Christmas.

"What would you like to do?" her mother asked.

"I want to place farolitos around Abuelo's grave," Luz said.

"That's a wonderful idea," her father replied.

Late in the afternoon they put on their coats and jackets and went to the cemetery. They put farolitos around her grandparents' graves.

Luz lit the candles. She prayed for her abuelo and thought of all the things they had done together.

"It looks beautiful," a woman said.

"I have extra bags and candles," Luz said, and she helped the woman place farolitos around the tombstone of her husband.

Luz's father went to the store for more bags and candles. Soon everybody was making the simple lanterns to place around the grave sites.

Across the cemetery hundreds of farolitos glowed brightly in the cold dusk. Some of the villagers gathered to sing Christmas carols. A woman who lived near the church brought a huge pot of hot chocolate and biscochitos to share.

"This is wonderful," Luz's mother said and hugged her daughter.

"Looks like you've started a new tradition," her father said.

"On Christmas Eve I will light farolitos for Abuelo, and in the spring I will plant his garden," Luz said to her parents. "Just like he said, Abuelo will always be with me."

AUTHOR'S NOTE

A tradition in New Mexico is to decorate one's home with farolitos during Christmas. The tradition comes from lighting bonfires (luminarias) at the entrance to the village church on Christmas Eve. The words *farolitos* and *luminarias* are often used interchangeably.

In my first children's book, *The Farolitos of Christmas*, I told how Luz discovered a way to make farolitos to help her grandfather keep a promise. In this story, Luz realizes, upon her grandfather's death, that she can place the farolitos around his grave site as a way of remembering the wonderful times they spent together.

In the Mexican tradition, *El Dia de los Muertos*, the Day of the Dead, is celebrated on November 1st and 2nd. Families go to the cemeteries to clean the grave sites, build altars, and take flowers and food offerings. It is one of the most important Mexican festivals.

In *Farolitos for Abuelo*, the idea of remembering the dead occurs on Christmas Eve. This tradition has grown in my hometown, and hundreds of people place farolitos at the cemetery. By nightfall thousands of these simple lanterns glow in the cold night as a celebration of joy and remembrance.—*R. A.*

GLOSSARY

abuelo	grandfather
biscochitos	traditional Christmas sugar cookies
buenos dias te de Dios	God give you a good day
buenas tardes	good afternoon
camposanto	cemetery
Los Pastores	a traditional nativity play
luminarias	small bonfires of stacked logs
mi'jita	my daughter, short for *mi hijita*
pastores	shepherds
posole	a hominy stew with meat
Sangre de Cristo Mountains	mountains of northern New Mexico
tortillas	flat, round bread